We Wanted You

by Liz Rosenberg · *paintings by Peter Catalanotto*

ROARING BROOK PRESS

Brookfield, Connecticut

From the moment you
were born—and even before that
moment—we knew we wanted you.

But we had to wait.
We didn't know where to find you.

We looked between the clouds

and the mountains

and the waves in the sea,

and then, just in case, we made
a quilt of pink and green and blue.

No baby came along tapping at our gate.

No baby slid down the chimney like Santa.

No baby peeked from under the cabbage leaves
in the garden.

So we waited, hopefully. And while we were
waiting, we fixed up an old rocking chair.
We painted a room.

I suppose you could say you came to us
through the telephone. That is, one day we got
a telephone call telling us to come. For you.

And so we came. We flew!

Because that's how much we wanted you.

Somewhere in the world a
mother gave birth to you,
a father gave life to you.
We weren't your first father
and mother.

But we waited
for you. We rocked
you in the middle of the night and sang
to you. When you cried, we came. When you
laughed for the first time, we clapped our hands. We
wrapped you up, tucked you in, and settled you down.

And that's how you know that you are really ours. Because we were yours, all along. We wanted you so much, back then.

We Love You, Enrique!

And we still do.

For Eli whom we wanted and are still grateful to each day—L.R.

For Marie Kruopas, Ginnette Maruschak, Amy Kallelis, Regina Skurnowicz, Jody, Elizabeth, & Tim—P.C.

Thanks to Paul and Jake, Chris and Karen, Emeterio and Erick, and especially Enrique.—P.C.

A Neal Porter Book
Text copyright © 2002 by Liz Rosenberg
Illustrations copyright © 2002 by Peter Catalanotto

Published by Roaring Brook Press
A division of The Millbrook Press, 2 Old New Milford Road, Brookfield, Connecticut 06804

Library of Congress Cataloging-in-Publication Data
Rosenberg, Liz
We Wanted You / by Liz Rosenberg ; illustrated by Peter Catalanotto.–1st ed.
p. cm.
Summary: Parents tell how they waited and prepared for the baby that they wanted so much.
[1. Parent and child–Fiction.   2. Adoption–Fiction.]   I. Catalanotto, Peter, ill.   II. Title.
PZ7.R71894 We 2002
[E]–dc21   98-047255

ISBN 0-7613-1597-7 (trade)   10 9 8 7 6 5 4 3 2 1
ISBN 0-7613-2661-8 (library binding)   10 9 8 7 6 5 4 3 2 1

Printed in Hong Kong

First Edition